Polar Bear Postman

by SEIGO KIJIMA

SHIROKUMA POST

MUSEYON
New York

This is Milk, the postmaster at the Polar Bear Post Office.
All the animals in the forest know they can count on him.

One morning, when Milk was stamping the mail, he noticed
a postcard that was addressed to him.

What's this? thought Milk.

Quickly he read the postcard.

Our baby chick has been missing for three days.

We got separated while we were looking for food together in the marsh.

We searched as soon as we realized he was missing, but we couldn't find him.

Please help us, Mr. Milk.

From the Red-Crowned Cranes
in District 1

"Oh my goodness! This is serious!" Milk exclaimed, and he rushed out of his post office.

Milk hurried to the red fox.
"Hello, Fox, my friend.
Sorry to bother you, but did you
happen to eat a red-crowned
crane chick?"

The red fox rubbed his sleepy
eyes. "A red-crowned crane
chick, you said?
Oh my, no, I haven't eaten one
in a long time. . . .

But why are you asking me that question?"

"Oh, no reason in particular. Goodbye."
Then Milk hurried to find the white-tailed eagle.

"Hello, Eagle, my friend. Sorry to bother you, but did you happen to eat a red-crowned crane chick?"

The white-tailed eagle's eyes glinted. "What? A red-crowned crane chick? They're delicious, aren't they? I wish I could have one. . . .

But why are you asking me that question?"

"Oh, no reason in particular. Goodbye."

Milk headed back to his post office.

He looked at the postcard from the mother and father crane again, put up a *Closed* sign, and went out.

Milk visited the crane parents in the swamp.
The mother and father looked exhausted and sad.
"We didn't want to leave in case our baby came home or needed us.
That's why we sent you the postcard. Please help us."

"Everything will be all right. We will find him," Milk said confidently.

Milk hurried to find the Siberian chipmunk.

"Milk, my friend. Is something wrong?"

Milk showed him the postcard from the red-crowned cranes.

"Wow, this is serious," said the Siberian chipmunk.

"I'll tell all my chipmunk buddies."

"Thank you. If you hear anything, please let me know at the post office."

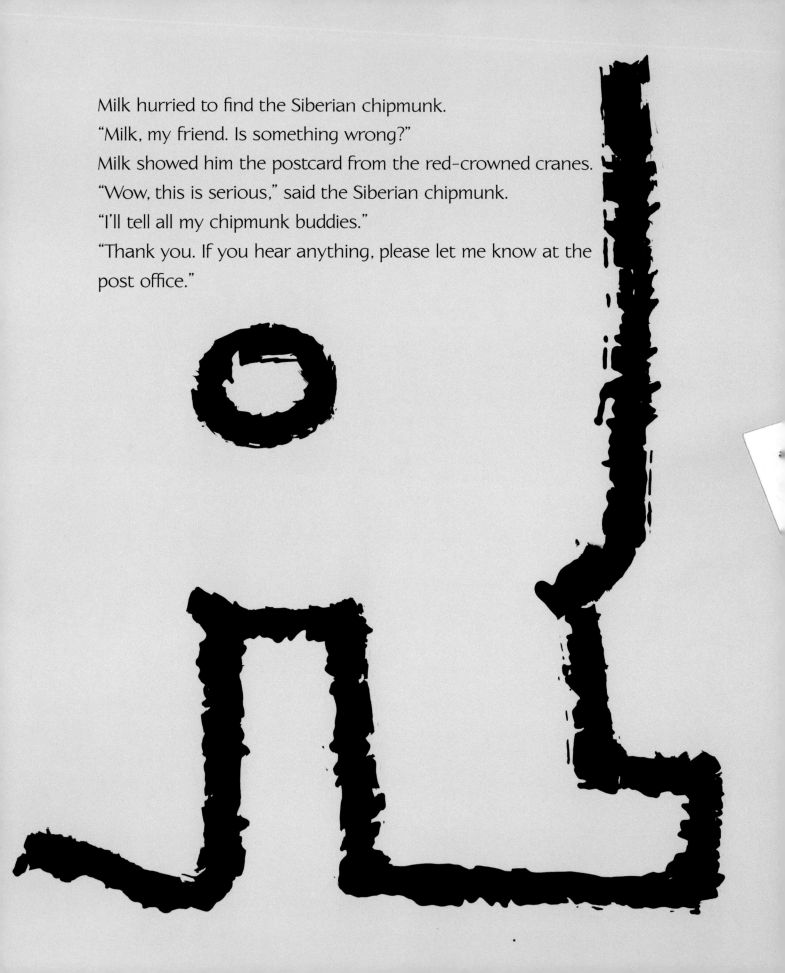

Milk went to the forest to see the sika deer.
"Oh my, it's Milk from the post office. Is something wrong?"
Milk showed her the postcard from the red-crowned cranes.
"My goodness, this is serious! I'll tell all my deer friends."

"Thank you. If you hear anything, please let me know at the post office."

That night, Milk went to visit the old Blakiston's
fish owl.
"Hoo, Milk! Is something wrong?"
Milk showed him the postcard from the red–
crowned cranes.
"Hooo! Hooo! This is serious. I'll tell my owl friends
right away."
"Thank you. If you hear anything, please let me
know at the post office."

Milk looked for the baby bird every day.
He waited for information from his friends.

Spring passed and summer came,
but there was no sign of the chick.

One morning, when Milk was stamping the mail,
he noticed a postcard that was addressed to him.

What's this? thought Milk. Quickly he read the postcard.

POST CARD

9 4 6 4 6 4 9

Mr. Milk
Polar Bear Post Office
PLEASE HELP!

At the beginning of spring, we found a red-crowned crane baby in the marsh.

We looked for his parents but could not find them.

We have taken care of the chick, and he is healthy and well.

His wings are strong, and it is almost time for him to fly.

We will miss him, but he should be with his own mother and father.

Please find his parents.

From the Red-Crowned Cranes
in District 3

WOW!!!
Milk was overjoyed.
He hurried to tell the
red-crowned crane
parents in District 1.

He shared the good
news with his friends
in the forest, too.

A few hours later, the mother and father crane from District 1
looked at their baby with tears in their eyes.
"Oh, how big and beautiful he has grown.
We will never let him out of our sight again."
They turned to the red-crowned cranes from District 3.
"Thank you for taking care of our child. We are so grateful
for what you did."
All the forest friends watched, happy and relieved,
as the red-crowned cranes from District 3 flew into the sky.

This is Milk, the postmaster at the Polar Bear Post Office.
He delivers happiness when he delivers the mail.

Polar Bear Postman

Shirokuma Yubinkyoku © 2015 Seigo Kijima

All rights reserved.

Publisher's Cataloging-in-Publication Data

Names: Kijima, Seigo, 1949- author, illustrator. | Gharbi, Mariko Shii, translator. | Kaplan, Simone, editor.

Title: Polar bear postman / by Seigo Kijima ; translation by Mariko Shii Gharbi ; English editing by Simone Kaplan ; US design and typography by Stephanie Bart-Horvath

Other titles: Shirokuma yubinkyoku. English.

Description: New York : Museyon, [2017] | "Originally published in Japan in 2015 by Poplar Publishing Co., Ltd."— Title page verso. | Audience: Ages 5-7. |

Identifiers: ISBN: 978-1-940842-09-7 | LCCN: 2017942149

Subjects: LCSH: Polar bear—Juvenile fiction. | Letter carriers—Juvenile fiction. | Postal service—Juvenile fiction. | Cranes (Birds)—Juvenile fiction. | Missing children—Juvenile fiction. | Picture books for children. | CYAC: Polar bear—Fiction. | Letter carriers—Fiction. | Postal service—Fiction.| Cranes (Birds)—Fiction. | Missing children—Fiction. | LCGFT: Picture books. | BISAC: JUVENILE FICTION / Animals / Bears.

Classification: LCC: PZ7.1.K55 P6513 2017 | DDC: [E]--dc23

Published in the United States by:
Museyon Inc.
1177 Avenue of the Americas, 5th Floor
New York, NY 10036

Museyon is a registered trademark.

Visit us online at www.museyon.com

Originally published in Japan in 2015 by Poplar Publishing Co., Ltd.

English translation rights arranged with Poplar Publishing Co., Ltd.

Printed in Shenzhen, China

ISBN 978-1-940842-21-9 • 0710150